P9-AQD-818

Macbeth

William Shakespeare

SADDLEBACK
EDUCATIONAL PUBLISHING

Saddleback's ***Illustrated Classics***™

Three Watson
Irvine, CA 92618-2767
Website: www.sdlback.com

ISBN-13: 978-1-59905-149-9
ISBN-10: 1-59905-149-4
eBook: 978-1-60291-179-6

Printed in China

12 11 10 09 08 9 8 7 6 5 4 3 2

Welcome to Saddleback's *Illustrated Classics*™

We are proud to welcome you to Saddleback's *Illustrated Classics*™. Saddleback's *Illustrated Classics*™ was designed specifically for the classroom to introduce readers to many of the great classics in literature. Each text, written and adapted by teachers and researchers, has been edited using the Dale-Chall vocabulary system. In addition, much time and effort has been spent to ensure that these high-interest stories retain all of the excitement, intrigue, and adventure of the original books.

With these graphically *Illustrated Classics*™, you learn what happens in the story in a number of different ways. One way is by reading the words a character says. Another way is by looking at the drawings of the character. The artist can tell you what kind of person a character is and what he or she is thinking or feeling.

This series will help you to develop confidence and a sense of accomplishment as you finish each novel. The stories in Saddleback's *Illustrated Classics*™ are fun to read. And remember, fun motivates!

Overview

Everyone deserves to read the best literature our language has to offer. Saddleback's *Illustrated Classics*™ was designed to acquaint readers with the most famous stories from the world's greatest authors, while teaching essential skills. You will learn how to:

- Establish a purpose for reading
- Activate prior knowledge
- Evaluate your reading
- Listen to the language as it is written
- Extend literary and language appreciation through discussion and writing activities.

Reading is one of the most important skills you will ever learn. It provides the key to all kinds of information. By reading the *Illustrated Classics*™, you will develop confidence and the self-satisfaction that comes from accomplishment—a solid foundation for any reader.

Remember,

"Today's readers are tomorrow's leaders."

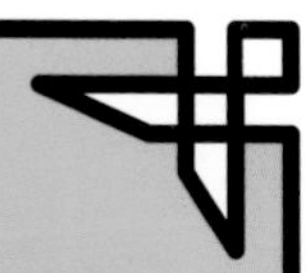

William Shakespeare

William Shakespeare was baptized on April 26, 1564, in Stratford-on-Avon, England, the third child of John Shakespeare, a well-to-do merchant, and Mary Arden, his wife. Young William probably attended the Stratford grammar school, where he learned English, Greek, and a great deal of Latin. Historians aren't sure of the exact date of Shakespeare's birth.

In 1582, Shakespeare married Anne Hathaway. By 1583 the couple had a daughter, Susanna, and two years later the twins, Hamnet and Judith. Somewhere between 1585 and 1592 Shakespeare went to London, where he became first an actor and then a playwright. His acting company, *The King's Men*, appeared most often in the *Globe* theater, a part of which Shakespeare himself owned.

In all, Shakespeare is believed to have written thirty-seven plays, several nondramatic poems, and a number of sonnets. In 1611 when he left the active life of the theater, he returned to Stratford and became a country gentleman, living in the second-largest house in town. For five years he lived a quiet life. Then, on April 23, 1616, William Shakespeare died and was buried in Trinity Church in Stratford. From his own time to the present, Shakespeare is considered one of the greatest writers of the English-speaking world.

William Shakespeare

Macbeth

BANQUO
3 WITCHES
MACDUFF
MACBETH
DUNCAN
LADY MACBETH

WHEN SHALL WE MEET AGAIN?
WHEN THE FIGHTING IS OVER.
THEN WE WILL MEET WITH MACBETH.
IN A LONELY SPOT IN SCOTLAND, THREE WITCHES MET TO MAKE THEIR EVIL PLANS. AROUND THEIR CAULDRON,* THEY SPOKE OF GOING TO SEE MACBETH, A GREAT GENERAL** WHO WAS AT THAT MOMENT FIGHTING IN A WAR AGAINST NORWAY.

* a large kettle

** an army officer of the highest rank

MANY MILES AWAY, KING DUNCAN OF SCOTLAND WAS IN AN ARMY CAMP.
IT IS HARD TO BELIEVE THAT SOME PEOPLE WOULD TURN AGAINST THEIR OWN KING!

GOOD KING DUNCAN WAS JOINED BY HIS TWO SONS, MALCOLM AND DONALBAIN.

ALSO AT THE KING'S SIDE WAS A NOBLEMAN* NAMED LENNOX AND MANY ROYAL ATTENDANTS.**

* a man of high rank, often an advisor to the king

** members of a king's court

A BLEEDING MAN WAS BROUGHT TO HIM FROM THE FIELD OF BATTLE.
THIS IS THE SERGEANT* WHO FOUGHT TO KEEP ME FROM BEING CAPTURED.**

TELL MY FATHER ABOUT THE BATTLE, FRIEND!

FOR A LONG TIME IT SEEMED THAT THE ENEMY AND THE KING'S FORCES WERE EQUALLY MATCHED.

"NEITHER ARMY COULD WIN AGAINST THE OTHER."

* an officer

** taken away by the enemy

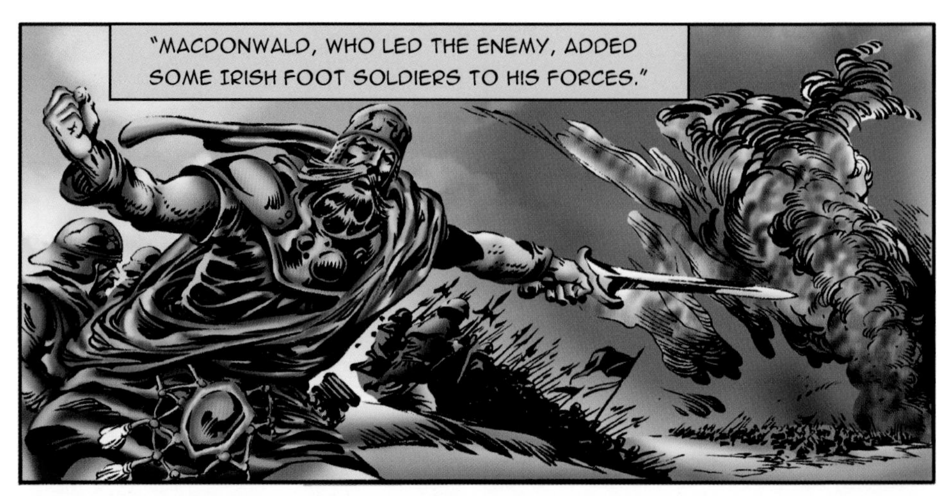
"MACDONWALD, WHO LED THE ENEMY, ADDED SOME IRISH FOOT SOLDIERS TO HIS FORCES."

"IT SEEMED THAT THE ENEMY MIGHT NOW BEGIN TO WIN OVER THE ARMY HEADED BY MACBETH AND BANQUO."

"BUT BRAVE MACBETH CHARGED* AND KILLED EVERYONE IN HIS PATH."

* went forward into battle

"AS HE FOUGHT, MACBETH FINALLY CAME UPON MACDONWALD."

"RAISING HIS SWORD HIGH IN THE AIR, MACBETH BROUGHT IT DOWN ON THE REBEL'S* CHEST."

"THEN HE CHOPPED OFF MACDON-WALD'S HEAD."

"WITHOUT A LEADER, THE REBELS RETREATED.** MACBETH HAD WON THE BATTLE!"

* a person who fights against the leaders of his own country

** moved back or away

"THEN HE WENT TO A NEARBY CASTLE TO REST. WHILE THERE, HE PUT MACDON-WALD'S HEAD ON THE CASTLE WALL TO STRIKE FEAR INTO THE REBELS' HEARTS.

"MEANWHILE, KING SWENO OF NORWAY ARRIVED WITH MORE SOLDIERS."
"GENERAL MACBETH AND BANQUO MARCHED AHEAD OF THEIR ARMY TO MEET THE NEW CHARGE."

BUT THE BRAVE SERGEANT COULD NOT FINISH HIS STORY.
FORGIVE ME, KING DUNCAN, BUT I FEAR I WILL FAINT. I CAN TALK NO MORE.

YOUR WOUNDS* MUST BE LOOKED AFTER. MY MEN WILL TAKE YOU TO THE DOCTOR.

JUST THEN TWO NOBLEMEN, ROSS AND ANGUS, ARRIVED. KING DUNCAN WAS EAGER** TO HEAR WHAT NEWS THEY BROUGHT.
WHERE HAVE YOU COME FROM?
FROM THE FIGHTING NEAR FIFE. MANY MEN WERE SENT AGAINST MACBETH AND HIS ARMY BY KING SWENO.

* injuries, cuts and gashes received while fighting

** anxious, looking forward to

"KING SWENO WAS HELPED BY THE THANE OF CAWDOR.* HE TURNED TRAITOR** TO SCOTLAND AND FOUGHT WITH THE NORWEGIANS AGAINST US."

"AGAIN IT SEEMED AS IF WE WOULD LOSE."

"THEN GENERAL MACBETH AND GOOD BANQUO TURNED THE TIDE OF BATTLE IN OUR FAVOR. KING SWENO AND THE REBELS WERE BEATEN."

* a Scottish title given to a trusted nobleman

** a person who joins forces with an enemy to fight against his own country

THAT IS GOOD NEWS, ROSS. THE WAR IS OVER.

I WILL SIGN A TREATY** WITH KING SWENO. BUT THE THANE OF CAWDOR MUST BE EXECUTED** FOR BEING A TRAITOR.

MACBETH MUST BE REWARDED FOR HIS GOOD WORK. I WILL MAKE HIM THE NEW THANE OF CAWDOR.
I'LL GO AND TELL MACBETH ABOUT THIS AT ONCE.

* a paper signed to end a war

** killed according to the law

MEANWHILE, NOW THAT THE FIGHTING WAS OVER, THE THREE WITCHES WAITED TO SPEAK WITH MACBETH AS HE LEFT THE BATTLE.

CROSSING THE HEATH,* MACBETH AND BANQUO CAME UPON THE WITCHES.
WHAT ARE YOU? SPEAK IF YOU CAN!

HAIL,** MACBETH, THANE OF GLAMIS!
HAIL, MACBETH, THANE OF CAWDOR!
HAIL, MACBETH, THE NEXT KING OF SCOTLAND!

* a stretch of marsh land covered with grass and low bushes

** a greeting

MACBETH, WHO WAS ALREADY THANE OF GLAMIS BUT DID NOT YET KNOW DUNCAN HAD NAMED HIM THANE OF CAWDOR, SHUDDERED* AT THE WITCHES' WORDS. HE KNEW THE ONLY WAY HE COULD BECOME KING WAS IF GOOD DUNCAN DIED.
DO NOT BE SO AFRAID, MACBETH. THEY HAVE NOT SAID ANYTHING TO HARM YOU.
THEN BANQUO TURNED AND ASKED THE WITCHES A QUESTION.
AND WHAT DO YOU SAY ABOUT *ME*?
YOU WILL NOT BE A KING, BUT YOU WILL BE THE FATHER OF KINGS.
WHEN THEY HAD FINISHED SPEAKING, ALL THREE WITCHES VANISHED** INTO THIN AIR.
WAIT! WHY DO YOU SAY THESE THINGS? YOU MUST TELL ME MORE!

* trembled, shook

** disappeared, went away

JUST THEN ROSS AND ANGUS DREW NEAR.
I HAVE GOOD NEWS FROM THE KING, MACBETH. YOU ARE TO BE THE NEW THANE OF CAWDOR.
HOW CAN HE DO THAT? THE THANE OF CAWDOR IS STILL ALIVE.

DUNCAN HAS ORDERED THE THANE EXECUTED FOR BEING A TRAITOR. THE KING HAS GIVEN YOU HIS TITLE.

MACBETH WAS STUNNED.* THE WITCHES' PREDICTIONS** WERE STARTING TO COME TRUE.
FRIEND BANQUO, WHAT DO YOU MAKE OF THIS? DOES IT PLEASE YOU THAT YOUR CHILDREN WILL BE KINGS?
I DON'T TRUST THE WITCHES, MACBETH.

* shocked, very surprised

** statements of future happenings

SOMETIMES, TO GET US TO DO WHAT IS WRONG, EVIL PEOPLE WILL TELL US SUCH THINGS.
BUT ONE OF THEIR PRE-DICTIONS HAS ALREADY COME TRUE!

I THANK YOU, ROSS AND ANGUS, FOR TELLING ME OF THIS. NOW LET US GO TO THE KING.

THINK ABOUT WHAT THE WITCHES HAVE SAID. WE WILL TALK ABOUT IT.

WHILE THESE THINGS WERE HAPPENING, KING DUNCAN WAITED FOR MACBETH IN HIS PALACE AT FORRES.
IS THE REBEL THANE OF CAWDOR EXECUTED YET?
YES, FATHER. HE DIED CONFESSING* HIS TREASON** AGAINST SCOTLAND.

SOON AFTER, MACBETH, BANQUO, ROSS AND ANGUS REACHED FORRES. THEY WENT TO SEE THE KING RIGHT AWAY.
MACBETH, MY COUSIN! I OWE YOU AND BANQUO MUCH FOR SAVING OUR COUNTRY. I SHALL REWARD YOU BOTH GREATLY.

NOW, BESIDES MAKING MACBETH THANE OF CAWDOR, I HAVE ANOTHER TITLE TO GIVE. MALCOLM, MY OLDEST SON, YOU ARE NOW THE PRINCE OF CUMBERLAND.
THEN I WILL BE THE NEXT KING OF SCOTLAND. THANK YOU, FATHER.

* admitting
** the act of being a traitor

I MUST HONOR YOU PROPERLY, MACBETH. WE WILL ALL GO TO VISIT YOUR CASTLE AT INVERNESS.
I AM GRATEFUL. I WILL GO AT ONCE TO TELL MY WIFE.

I MUST DO SOMETHING ABOUT THE PRINCE OF CUMBERLAND. HOW CAN I BE THE NEXT KING WHEN YOUNG MALCOLM STANDS IN MY WAY?

MEANWHILE, AT MACBETH'S CASTLE, LADY MACBETH READ A LETTER FROM HER HUSBAND.
MACBETH SAYS THAT THREE WITCHES PREDICTED HE WOULD BE THE THANE OF CAWDOR. . . AND THIS HAS COME TRUE!

THEY ALSO SAID HE WOULD BE KING. BUT I KNOW MY HUSBAND. HE WOULDN'T DO ANYTHING WRONG—EVEN TO WIN A CROWN!

SUDDENLY A MESSENGER ARRIVED WITH EXCITING NEWS.

MY LADY, KING DUNCAN IS ON HIS WAY TO INVERNESS!
THAT COULD NOT BE! MACBETH WOULD HAVE TOLD ME ABOUT IT!

NO, MY LADY. HE SENT A MESSENGER AHEAD, AND HE RIDES TO THE CASTLE EVEN NOW.
MY HUSBAND WILL ARRIVE SOON. AND AFTER THAT—KING DUNCAN!

THERE IS ONLY ONE THING TO DO. DUNCAN MUST DIE!

I MUST BE STRONG ENOUGH TO CARRY OUT THESE PLANS. NOTHING MUST STOP ME!

JUST THEN MACBETH ARRIVED AT INVERNESS. HE RUSHED TO SEE HIS WIFE.
GREETINGS TO YOU, MY HUSBAND, THANE OF BOTH GLAMIS AND CAWDOR!

MY DEAREST LOVE, THE KING COMES HERE TONIGHT!

AND WHEN DOES HE PLAN TO LEAVE?
TOMORROW.

THEN HE MUST NEVER SEE TOMORROW! MEANWHILE, MY HUSBAND, PREPARE TO WELCOME HIM. LEAVE EVERYTHING *ELSE* TO ME.

DO NOT WORRY. TONIGHT YOU SHALL WIN THE THRONE OF SCOTLAND.

WE WILL TALK MORE ABOUT THIS LATER.

SOON AFTERWARD, KING DUNCAN AND HIS MEN MADE THEIR WAY TO INVERNESS.
I LIKE THIS CASTLE. THE AIR IS SWEET AND GENTLE.

AH, IT IS LADY MACBETH. BUT WHERE IS YOUR NOBLE HUSBAND?
HE IS WAITING INSIDE, SIR.

THEN LET US GO TO MEET HIM.

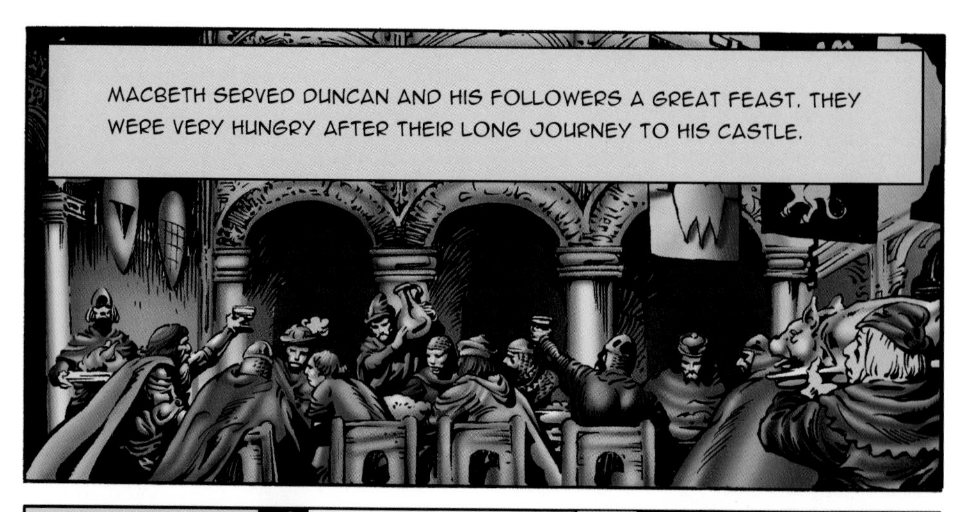
MACBETH SERVED DUNCAN AND HIS FOLLOWERS A GREAT FEAST. THEY WERE VERY HUNGRY AFTER THEIR LONG JOURNEY TO HIS CASTLE.

MACBETH'S THOUGHTS TROUBLED HIM. HE LEFT THE TABLE. LADY MACBETH WAS WORRIED AND FOLLOWED HER HUSBAND OUTSIDE. LADY MACBETH FOUND HIM THERE.
MACBETH! WHY DID YOU LEAVE THE TABLE? DO YOU WANT THE KING TO SUSPECT* SOMETHING?
I DON'T THINK THAT WE SHOULD GO THROUGH WITH THIS. DUNCAN IS MY COUSIN AND A GUEST IN MY HOUSE!

BUT *YOU* WERE THE ONE WHO FIRST THOUGHT OF KILLING DUNCAN FOR HIS CROWN!

I'LL GET DUNCAN'S GUARDS DRUNK TONIGHT. THEN YOU CAN STAB THE KING WHILE HE SLEEPS.

* begin to believe that something is wrong

LATER, AFTER THE FEAST, BANQUO'S SON FLEANCE WALKED IN THE CASTLE COURTYARD.
IT IS A DARK NIGHT, FATHER. WHY DON'T YOU GO TO BED?
I CANNOT, FLEANCE. MY SLEEP IS BOTHERED BY BAD DREAMS.

SUDDENLY BANQUO HEARD THE SOUND OF FOOTSTEPS, AND HE DREW HIS SWORD.

WHO'S THERE?

A FRIEND.

MACBETH! YOU'RE NOT IN BED YET? I DON'T SLEEP WELL, EITHER. I DREAMED OF THE THREE WITCHES LAST NIGHT.

I DON'T THINK ABOUT THEM MUCH. BUT YOU AND I MUST TALK ABOUT THEM LATER.
ANY TIME, MACBETH. GOODNIGHT.

MACBETH WAITED OUTSIDE IN THE COURTYARD UNTIL HIS WIFE HAD MADE THE KING'S GUARDS DRUNK.

SUDDENLY A GHOSTLY* DAGGER** APPEARED BEFORE MACBETH.
IS THIS A DAGGER WHICH I SEE BEFORE ME?

ITS HANDLE POINTS AT ME, BUT I CANNOT TOUCH IT.

* something which seems to appear, but which does not really exist

** a sharp knife

JUST THEN A BELL SOUNDED. IT WAS THE SIGNAL FROM LADY MACBETH THAT EVERYTHING WAS READY.
BONG BONG BONG
THERE'S THE BELL. I GO NOW TO SEND DUNCAN TO ANOTHER LIFE.

OUTSIDE THE KING'S ROOM, MACBETH MET HIS WIFE.
THE GUARDS ARE SOUND ASLEEP. TAKE THEIR DAGGERS AND STAB THE KING. I'LL WAIT HERE.

CLUTCHING* THE KNIVES, MAC-BETH ENTERED DUNCAN'S ROOM. SOON AFTERWARD HE RETURNED, THE DAGGERS DRIPPING WITH BLOOD.
IT IS DONE, MY WIFE. DUNCAN IS DEAD!

* holding tightly

BUT WHO SLEEPS IN THE ROOM NEXT TO THE KING'S?
HIS SON DONALBAIN. WHY DO YOU ASK?
"AS I STABBED DUNCAN, A VOICE CRIED OUT TO ME. . ."
MACBETH SHALL SLEEP NO MORE!
WELL, I DIDN'T HEAR ANYTHING. YOU MUST GO BACK AND LEAVE THE BLOODY KNIVES INSIDE.
NO! I DARE NOT LOOK AT DUNCAN'S DEAD BODY AGAIN! I'M AFRAID TO THINK ABOUT WHAT I HAVE DONE!

HERE, GIVE ME THE DAGGERS. I WILL DO IT FOR YOU.

LADY MACBETH TOOK THE DAGGERS FROM HER HUSBAND. SHE WENT INTO THE KING'S BEDROOM, PUT THE DAGGERS INTO THE SLEEPING GUARDS' HANDS, AND SMEARED THEIR FACES WITH BLOOD.

MEANWHILE, MACBETH LOOKED DOWN AT HIS BLOODY HANDS.

IT WOULD TAKE AN *OCEAN* TO WASH AWAY THIS BLOOD!

WHEN LADY MACBETH RETURNED, HER HANDS WERE AS RED AS HER HUSBAND'S.

LET US GO NOW, MACBETH. BOTH OF US MUST WASH, THEN GET READY FOR BED.

WALKING TO THEIR ROOM, MACBETH BEGAN TO FEEL SORRY THAT HE HAD MURDERED DUNCAN.

I HAVE DONE AN EVIL THING. HOW WILL I EVER BE ABLE TO LIVE WITH THAT THOUGHT?

THE FOLLOWING MORNING, LENNOX AND MACDUFF WENT EARLY TO THE CASTLE. AN OLD PORTER* LET THEM IN.
IS MACBETH AWAKE YET? WE ARE HERE TO SEE HIM.
I'LL CALL MY MASTER FOR YOU, GOOD SIRS.

* a servant who guards the gates and doors to his master's house

IN A FEW MO-MENTS, MACBETH ENTERED THE ROOM.
GOOD MORNING, GENTLEMEN.
GREETINGS, GOOD THANE. WE HAVE BUSINESS WITH THE KING. IS HE UP YET?

WHY, NO. BUT HIS ROOM IS JUST DOWN THE HALL. I'LL BRING YOU TO HIM.
DO NOT TROUBLE YOURSELF, MACBETH. *I'LL* WAKE HIM UP.

MACDUFF KNOCKED AND THEN OPENED KING DUNCAN'S DOOR. A LOOK OF TERROR* WAS ON HIS FACE AND HE CRIED OUT IN ALARM.
MURDER! TREASON! MURDER!

* fright, fear

MACDUFF'S LOUD SHOUTS WOKE EVERYONE IN THE CASTLE.
WHAT A TERRIBLE THING! KING DUNCAN IS DEAD!
WHAT? IN OUR *OUR* HOUSE? I AM GOING TO FAINT!

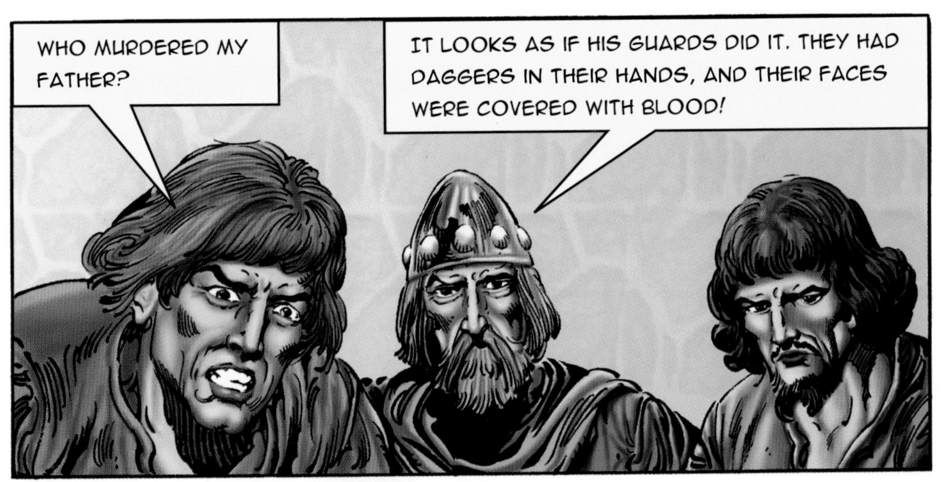
WHO MURDERED MY FATHER?
IT LOOKS AS IF HIS GUARDS DID IT. THEY HAD DAGGERS IN THEIR HANDS, AND THEIR FACES WERE COVERED WITH BLOOD!

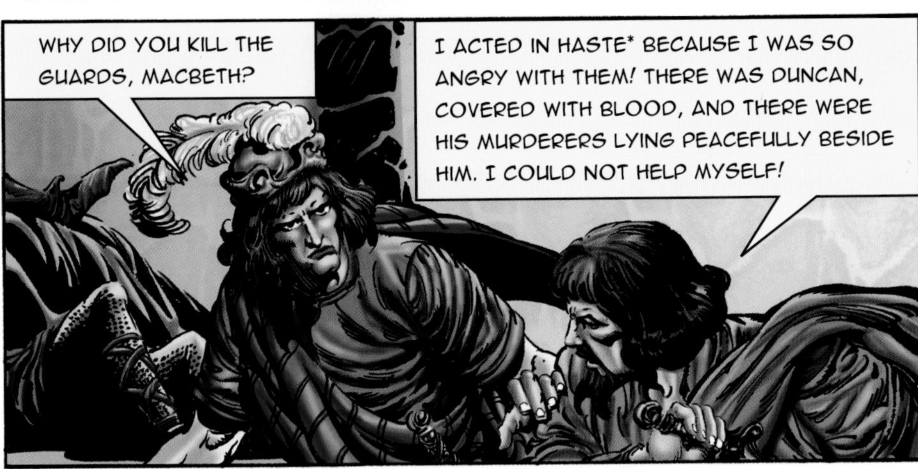
WHY DID YOU KILL THE GUARDS, MACBETH?
I ACTED IN HASTE* BECAUSE I WAS SO ANGRY WITH THEM! THERE WAS DUNCAN, COVERED WITH BLOOD, AND THERE WERE HIS MURDERERS LYING PEACEFULLY BESIDE HIM. I COULD NOT HELP MYSELF!

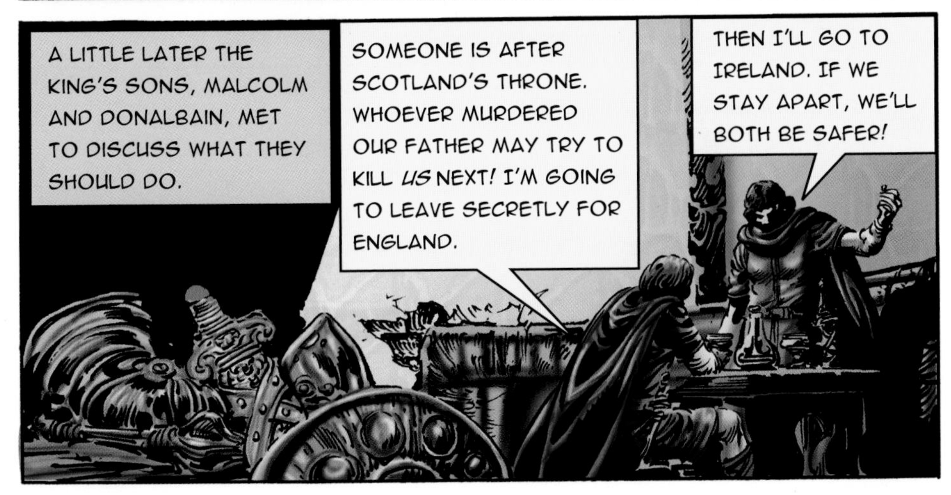
A LITTLE LATER THE KING'S SONS, MALCOLM AND DONALBAIN, MET TO DISCUSS WHAT THEY SHOULD DO.
SOMEONE IS AFTER SCOTLAND'S THRONE. WHOEVER MURDERED OUR FATHER MAY TRY TO KILL *US* NEXT! I'M GOING TO LEAVE SECRETLY FOR ENGLAND.
THEN I'LL GO TO IRELAND. IF WE STAY APART, WE'LL BOTH BE SAFER!

* too quickly

SEVERAL HOURS LATER, ROSS AND MACDUFF SPOKE ABOUT DUNCAN'S DEATH.
DOES ANYONE KNOW WHO ORDERED THE GUARDS TO STAB THE KING?
NO, BUT MALCOLM AND DONALBAIN HAVE BOTH LEFT SCOTLAND.

IT LOOKS BAD THAT DUNCAN'S SONS HAVE RUN AWAY. PERHAPS THEY DID IT.
THAT MEANS MACBETH WILL BE THE NEXT KING.

WILL YOU GO TO SCONE TO SEE HIM CROWNED?
NO, I DON'T FEEL RIGHT ABOUT IT. I AM GOING HOME TO CASTLE FIFE. FAREWELL.

NOT LONG AFTERWARD, MACBETH BECAME KING OF SCOTLAND. HE DECIDED TO HOLD A GREAT FEAST TO CELEBRATE. MANY NOBLES WERE INVITED TO THE ROYAL PALACE AT FORRES.

BANQUO WAITED FOR MACBETH INSIDE THE PALACE.
MACBETH HAS GAINED EVERYTHING THE WITCHES SAID HE WOULD. BUT I FEAR IT WAS HE WHO KILLED DUNCAN TO TAKE THE CROWN.

TRUMPETS SOUNDED, AND KING MACBETH ENTERED WITH SEVERAL MEMBERS OF HIS ROYAL COURT.
BANQUO, MY FRIEND, WE FEAST TONIGHT. WILL YOU JOIN US?
YES, SIR. BUT I PROMISED MY SON FLEANCE THAT WE WOULD GO HORSEBACK RIDING THIS AFTERNOON. WE WILL RETURN IN THE EVENING.

SOON BANQUO AND THE OTHER NOBLES HAD LEFT. MACBETH SAT ALONE, WORRYING AND THINKING.
THE WITCHES SAID THAT BANQUO WOULD BE THE FATHER OF KINGS. HE IS A THREAT* TO MY THRONE. I MUST KILL *HIM* TOO!

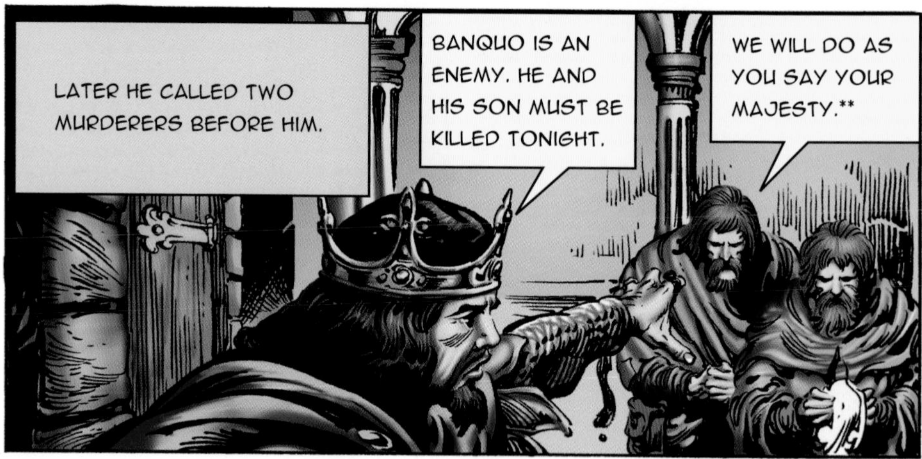
LATER HE CALLED TWO MURDERERS BEFORE HIM.
BANQUO IS AN ENEMY. HE AND HIS SON MUST BE KILLED TONIGHT.
WE WILL DO AS YOU SAY YOUR MAJESTY.**

WHEN THE MURDERERS HAD GONE, LADY MACBETH CAME IN TO TALK TO HER HUSBAND.
DO NOT WORRY SO ABOUT WHAT WE HAVE DONE. IT'S FINISHED!
NO, NOT YET. TONIGHT ANOTHER MURDER WILL BE DONE. WHEN IT IS OVER, I WILL TELL YOU ABOUT IT.

* a warning of some future evil

** a title given to a king

LATER THAT EVENING, THE KILLERS WAITED FOR BANQUO AND HIS SON TO RETURN FROM THEIR RIDE. A THIRD MAN HAD JOINED THEM AT MACBETH'S ORDERS.
I SEE A LIGHT. THEY ARE COMING!

THE MURDERERS STRUCK AT BANQUO WITH THEIR SWORDS, BUT YOUNG FLEANCE WAS TOO FAST FOR THEM.
I'M BEING ATTACKED! GET AWAY WHILE YOU CAN, MY SON!

WE GOT THE FATHER, BUT THE SON ESCAPED. WE LEFT THE MOST IMPORTANT PART UNDONE!
WELL, LET'S GO AND TELL THE KING WHAT HAPPENED.

MEANWHILE, NOT FAR AWAY, MACBETH'S FEAST HAD BEGUN.
YOU ARE ALL WELCOME HERE! PLEASE FIND A PLACE TO SIT AT THE TABLE.

THE QUEEN WILL JOIN US A LITTLE LATER.

AS THE FEASTING STARTED, MACBETH SAW ONE OF THE KILLERS IN THE DOORWAY.

THERE IS BLOOD ON YOUR FACE!
IT IS BANQUO'S BLOOD! HE IS DEAD IN A DITCH WITH TWENTY GASHES IN HIS HEAD!

AND WHAT OF FLEANCE?
I AM SORRY TO REPORT THAT THE BOY HAS ESCAPED.

WELL, THE MAIN JOB IS DONE. WE'LL TAKE CARE OF FLEANCE ANOTHER TIME. FOR NOW, YOU MAY LEAVE.

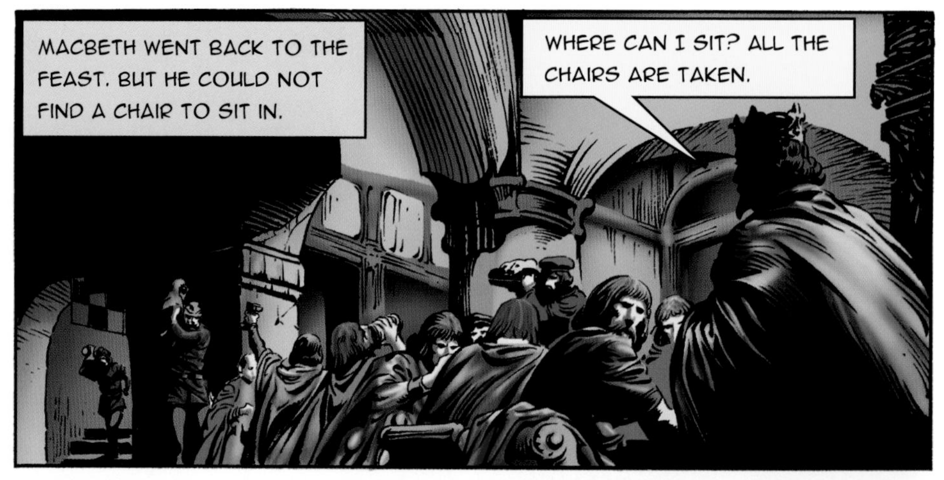
MACBETH WENT BACK TO THE FEAST. BUT HE COULD NOT FIND A CHAIR TO SIT IN.
WHERE CAN I SIT? ALL THE CHAIRS ARE TAKEN.

WHY, RIGHT HERE, YOUR MAJESTY.

BUT BANQUO'S GHOST WAS SITTING IN THE EMPTY SEAT.
NO! WHICH OF YOU HAS DONE THIS?

YOU CANNOT SAY I DID IT! DON'T SHAKE YOUR BLOODY HEAD AT ME!

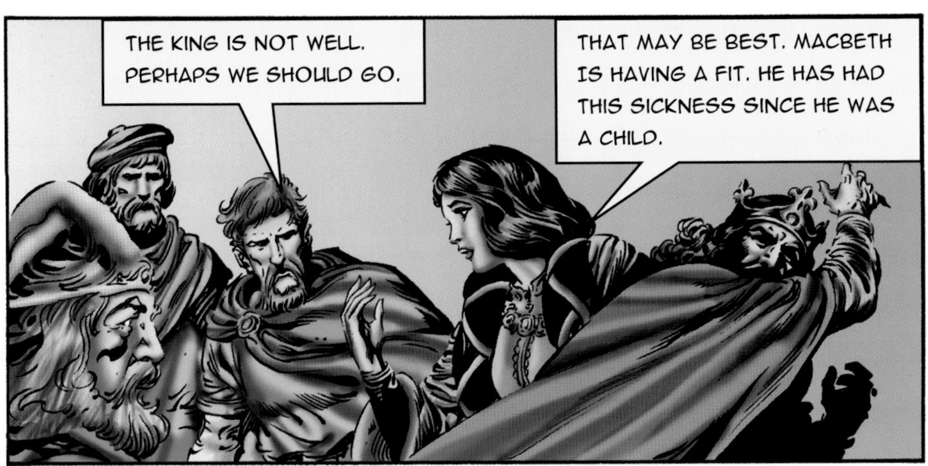
THE KING IS NOT WELL. PERHAPS WE SHOULD GO.
THAT MAY BE BEST. MACBETH IS HAVING A FIT. HE HAS HAD THIS SICKNESS SINCE HE WAS A CHILD.

I'LL TAKE CARE OF HIM. PLEASE GENTLEMEN, LEAVE AT ONCE!

I HAVE BLOOD ON MY HANDS AND STRANGE THINGS IN MY MIND. I MUST TALK TO THE WITCHES AGAIN!
THEN DO IT TOMORROW. YOU NEED YOUR SLEEP, MY HUSBAND.

EARLY THE NEXT DAY WHEN MACBETH HAD LEFT THE CASTLE, LENNOX TALKED WITH A FRIEND ABOUT THE RECENT* HAPPENINGS.

I HEAR THAT MACDUFF IS IN TROUBLE WITH THE KING. MACDUFF SAYS BAD THINGS BECAUSE HE REFUSED TO ATTEND LAST NIGHT'S FEAST. WHERE IS HE?
DIDN'T YOU KNOW, LENNOX? MACDUFF WENT TO SEE KING EDWARD OF ENGLAND. PRINCE MALCOLM IS THERE TOO.

MACDUFF WANTS KING EDWARD TO ORDER SIWARD, THE EARL OF NORTHUMBERLAND, TO HELP MALCOLM OVERTHROW** MACBETH! EVERYONE IS SURE NOW THAT MACBETH WAS THE ONE WHO MURDERED GOOD KING DUNCAN!

MACDUFF HAS BEEN ORDERED TO RETURN TO SCOTLAND, BUT HE WILL NOT OBEY.

* not long ago

** win a battle against someone and take his place

MEANWHILE, MACBETH HAD FOUND THE CAVE OF THE THREE WITCHES.
I NEED YOUR HELP, WOMEN! SHOW ME MY FUTURE!
VERY WELL, MACBETH. HERE IT IS.

THE FIRST WITCH CONJURED* UP A HEAD THAT SPOKE.
BEWARE MACDUFF, THE THANE OF FIFE!

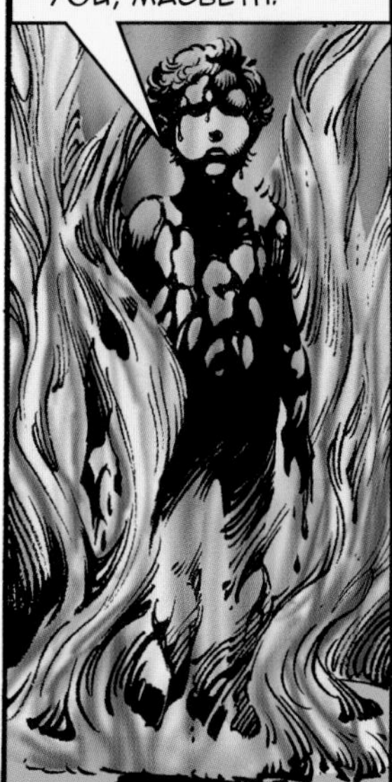
A SECOND VISION** APPEARED. IT TOOK THE FORM OF A BLOODY CHILD.
NO ONE BORN OF A WOMAN CAN HARM YOU, MACBETH!

THEN THE GHOST OF A SMALL CHILD CAME INTO VIEW. IT HAD A CROWN ON ITS HEAD AND IT HELD A TREE BRANCH IN ONE HAND.
YOU WILL NEVER BE DEFEATED UNTIL BIRNAM WOOD MARCHES TO DUNSINANE HILL!

* called up by magic

** a picture or object that exists only in the mind of the one who sees it

MACBETH WAS HAPPY WITH THE VISIONS, BUT HE WANTED TO KNOW MORE. HE WAS STILL TROUBLED BY THE WITCHES' PROPHECY* THAT BANQUO WOULD BE THE FATHER OF KINGS. THE THREE OLD HAGS SHOWED MACBETH THAT THEIR WORDS WOULD COME TRUE.

THAT FIRST MAN—THAT'S *BANQUO!* AND ALL THE OTHERS LOOK JUST LIKE HIM. YES, HE POINTS HIS FINGER AT THEM TO SHOW ME THEY ARE HIS. THIS IS AN EVIL DAY!

* telling what will happen in the future

WHY DOES MACBETH LOOK ANGRY? WE'VE DONE OUR BEST TO CHEER HIM UP!

AS THE WITCHES DISAPPEARED, LENNOX CAME INTO THE CAVE LOOKING FOR MACBETH.
THE THREE WITCHES ARE GONE, LENNOX. DID YOU SEE WHERE THEY WENT?
NO, SIR. BUT I HAVE NEWS FOR YOU ABOUT THANE MACDUFF. HE HAS FLED TO ENGLAND!

I MUST ACT QUICKLY TO PUNISH HIM! I WILL SEND SOLDIERS TO HIS CASTLE TO MURDER HIS WIFE AND CHILDREN.

MEANWHILE, ROSS WAS TRYING TO COMFORT LADY MACDUFF WHO COULD NOT UNDERSTAND WHY HER HUSBAND HAD RUN AWAY.

MACDUFF ACTS LIKE A TRAITOR!

NO. YOUR HUSBAND IS WISE. HE KNOWS WHAT IS BEST FOR SCOTLAND.

SOON AFTERWARD, ROSS LEFT TO JOIN MACDUFF IN ENGLAND, LEAVING LADY MACDUFF IN TEARS.

WHY ARE YOU CRYING, MOTHER?
YOUR FATHER IS GONE. I DON'T KNOW HOW WE WILL LIVE WITHOUT HIM!

MOMENTS LATER, A MESSENGER ARRIVED WITH A WARNING THAT MACBETH'S MEN WERE ON THEIR WAY.

YOUR LIVES ARE IN DANGER! YOU MUST GET AWAY FROM HERE!

WHY? WE HAVE DONE NOTHING WRONG.

BUT THERE WAS NO TIME TO EXPLAIN. MACBETH'S SOLDIERS FORCED THEIR WAY IN AND KILLED LADY MACDUFF AND HER SON.

MEANWHILE, ON HIS WAY TO ENGLAND, ROSS HAD LEARNED ABOUT THE DEATH OF LADY MACDUFF. ARRIVING AT KING EDWARD'S PALACE, HE FOUND MACDUFF TALKING WITH DUNCAN'S SON MALCOLM.
HAIL, ROSS. HOW IS SCOTLAND?
MACBETH IS A MADMAN. THE WHOLE COUNTRY SUFFERS.

DON'T WORRY, ROSS. ENGLAND HAS GIVEN US SIWARD, THE EARL OF NORTHUMBERLAND, ALONG WITH TEN THOUSAND FIGHTING MEN.
WE WILL SOON GO TO WAR TO SAVE SCOTLAND FROM MACBETH.

THEN, KNOWING HE COULD NOT PUT IT OFF ANY LONGER, ROSS TOLD MACDUFF ABOUT HIS WIFE AND SON.
WHAT? MACBETH HAS SLAIN MY FAMILY? I WILL KILL HIM IN RETURN!

MEANWHILE, BACK IN SCOTLAND, ONE OF LADY MACBETH'S SER-VANTS CALLED A DOCTOR.
WHEN WAS THE LAST TIME LADY MACBETH WALKED IN HER SLEEP?
SHE HAS WALKED EVERY NIGHT SINCE MACBETH LEFT THE CASTLE TO PREPARE FOR WAR. LOOK! THERE SHE IS AGAIN!

LADY MACBETH WAS WALKING IN HER SLEEP WITH HER EYES WIDE OPEN. AS THE DOC-TOR AND THE SERVANT WATCHED, SHE RUBBED HER HANDS TOGETH-ER AS IF SHE WERE WASHING THEM—OVER AND OVER AGAIN.
WILL THESE HANDS *NEVER* BE CLEAN? WHO WOULD HAVE THOUGHT THE OLD MAN HAD SO MUCH BLOOD IN HIM?

SHE WILL SOON GO BACK TO BED. CAN YOU HELP HER, DOCTOR?
NO, I CAN DO NOTHING. BUT KEEP AN EYE ON HER. SHE MIGHT TRY TO HURT HERSELF!

NOT LONG AFTERWARD, SCOTLAND WAS READY FOR WAR. MANY NOBLEMEN REVOLTED* AGAINST MACBETH AND PLANNED TO ATTACK HIM.
THE ENGLISH TROOPS LED BY MALCOLM, SIWARD, AND MACDUFF ARE NEAR.
YES, THEY ARE AT BIRNAM WOOD. WE WILL MEET THEM THERE.

MACBETH GATHERS HIS FORCES AT CASTLE DUNSINANE. HE IS LIKE A MADMAN!
HIS SOLDIERS ONLY FOLLOW HIM OUT OF FEAR, NOT OUT OF LOVE!

COME. LET US MARCH TO BIRNAM AND JOIN THE ENGLISH SOLDIERS.

* turned against

BACK AT DUNSINANE CASTLE, MACBETH WAS NOT WORRIED. HE BELIEVED THAT THE WITCHES' PROPHECY WOULD KEEP HIM SAFE.
BIRNAM WOOD CANNOT WALK. AND NO MAN BORN OF A WOMAN CAN HARM ME. I HAVE NOTHING TO FEAR—NOT EVEN MACDUFF!

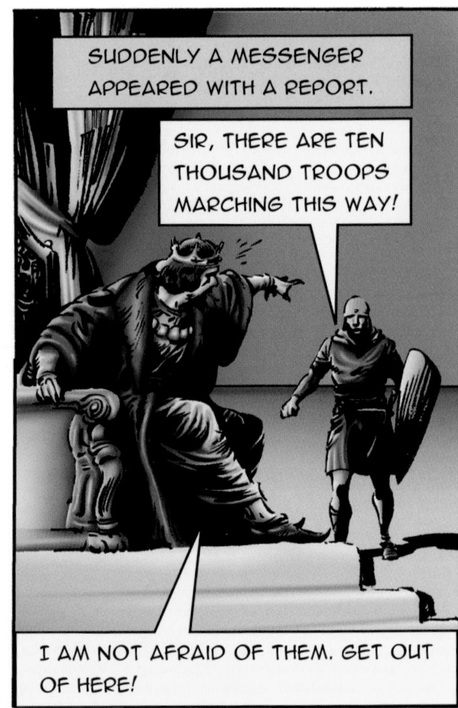
SUDDENLY A MESSENGER APPEARED WITH A REPORT.
SIR, THERE ARE TEN THOUSAND TROOPS MARCHING THIS WAY!
I AM NOT AFRAID OF THEM. GET OUT OF HERE!

WISELY, HOWEVER, MACBETH DECIDED TO DRESS FOR BATTLE.
HELP ME WITH MY ARMOR, SEYTON. IT IS EARLY YET, BUT I WISH TO BE READY ONCE THE FIGHTING STARTS.
YES, SIR.

SOON THE ENGLISH ARMY AND THE TROOPS FROM SCOTLAND MET AT BIRNAM WOOD.

ORDER EVERY SOLDIER TO CUT OFF A BRANCH AND CARRY IT. THAT WAY WE CAN DISGUISE* OUR TRUE NUMBERS FROM MACBETH.
IT SHALL BE DONE, SIR!

NOW WE ARE READY TO FIGHT MACBETH AT DUNSINANE!

* hide by taking on another appearance

ALL THIS TIME AT DUNSINANE, MACBETH THOUGHT MALCOLM, SIWARD, AND MACDUFF WERE HELPLESS AGAINST HIM.
HANG OUR BANNERS AND FLAGS FROM THE WALLS. CASTLE DUNSINANE IS STRONGER THAN THE ENEMY.

BUT THERE WAS TROUBLE IN HIS OWN HOUSE. SUDDENLY MACBETH HEARD THE SCREAMS OF WOMEN.
WHAT IS HAPPENING, SEYTON?
YOUR WIFE IS DEAD, SIR.

BUT MACBETH HAD LITTLE TIME TO MOURN.* JUST THEN A MESSENGER CAME IN WITH A STRANGE STORY.
SIR—THIS SOUNDS CRAZY. . . BUT WHEN I LOOKED OUT OVER THE CASTLE WALLS TOWARD BIRNAM WOOD, IT SEEMED TO ME THAT THE TREES WERE WALKING UP THE HILL!

* cry, feel bad about something

YOU'RE LYING!
NO, SIR. YOU CAN SEE IT FOR YOURSELF!

AT THIS, MACBETH REMEMBERED THE WITCHES' PREDICTION.
THE WITCHES SAID I HAD NOTHING TO FEAR UNTIL BIRNAM WOOD COMES TO DUNSINANE. AND NOW THE FOREST WALKS THIS WAY!

MACBETH CALLED EVERYONE IN HIS CASTLE TO BATTLE.
GET YOUR WEAPONS! WE WILL MEET THE ENEMY OUTSIDE. IF WE MUST DIE, WE WILL DIE FIGHTING!

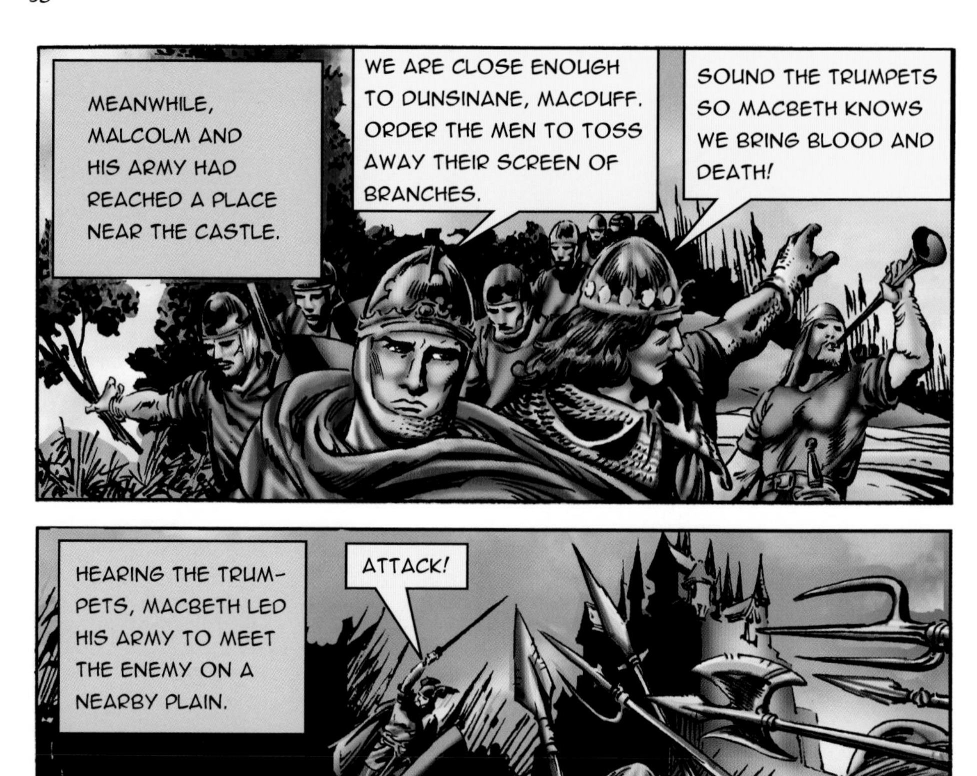
MEANWHILE, MALCOLM AND HIS ARMY HAD REACHED A PLACE NEAR THE CASTLE.
WE ARE CLOSE ENOUGH TO DUNSINANE, MACDUFF. ORDER THE MEN TO TOSS AWAY THEIR SCREEN OF BRANCHES.
SOUND THE TRUMPETS SO MACBETH KNOWS WE BRING BLOOD AND DEATH!
HEARING THE TRUM-PETS, MACBETH LED HIS ARMY TO MEET THE ENEMY ON A NEARBY PLAIN.
ATTACK!

DURING THE BATTLE, SIWARD'S SON CHALLENGED* MACBETH TO A SWORDFIGHT.
WHAT IS YOUR NAME?
YOU WILL TREMBLE** TO HEAR IT. I AM MACBETH!

* dared

** shake with fear

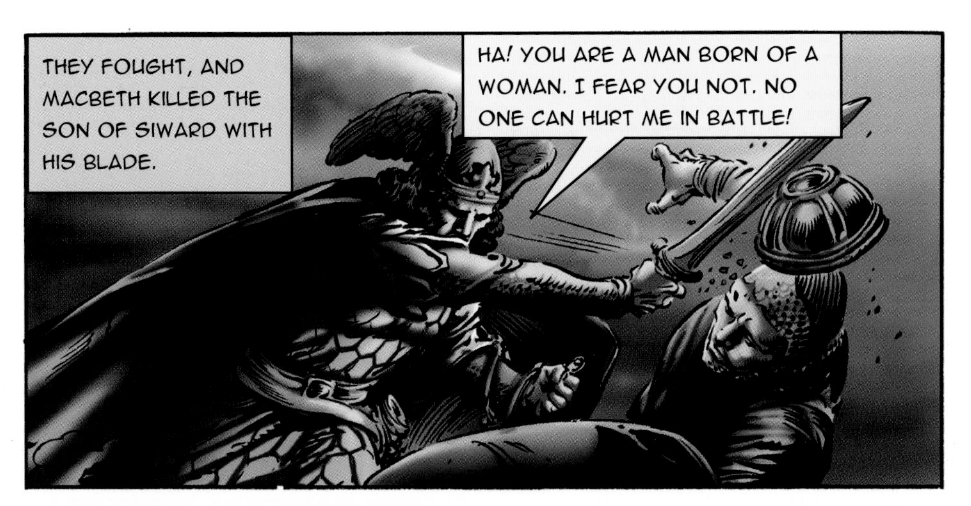
THEY FOUGHT, AND MACBETH KILLED THE SON OF SIWARD WITH HIS BLADE.
HA! YOU ARE A MAN BORN OF A WOMAN. I FEAR YOU NOT. NO ONE CAN HURT ME IN BATTLE!

MEANWHILE, MACDUFF SEARCHED EVERYWHERE FOR MACBETH.
WHERE IS THE KING? IF I DO NOT FIND HIM, MY DEAD FAMILY WILL HAUNT* ME FOREVER.

NEARBY, MALCOLM AND SIWARD RODE INTO MACBETH'S CASTLE.
MANY OF MACBETH'S OWN TROOPS HAVE DESERTED** HIM AND JOINED US. DUNSINANE IS OURS!

* in this sense, to make someone ashamed for not getting revenge

** left, went over to the other side

AFTER MUCH FIGHT-ING, MACDUFF FOUND MACBETH ON THE BATTLEFIELD.
MACBETH! TAKE UP YOUR SWORD AND FIGHT ME!
YOU CANNOT DEFEAT ME, MACDUFF. MY LIFE IS CHARMED.* NO ONE BORN OF A WOMAN CAN KILL!

I HAVE ALREADY KILLED YOUR FAM-ILY. I HAVE NO WISH TO ADD YOUR BLOOD TO MY HANDS. GET AWAY WHILE YOU STILL CAN, MACDUFF.
IT IS *YOU* WHO WILL DIE MACBETH!

MY MOTHER COULD NOT GIVE BIRTH TO ME IN THE USUAL WAY. THE DOCTOR CUT HER OPEN AND TOOK ME OUT. SO I WAS NOT REALLY "BORN," MACBETH!
I AM SORRY TO HEAR THIS.

* protected by magic

BUT I WILL NEVER GIVE UP!

THEREFORE WE MUST FIGHT!

COME ON, MACDUFF. THE ONE WHO STOPS FIRST WILL BE THE LOSER!

MEANWHILE MALCOLM'S ARMY HAD FINISHED FIGHTING. THEY HAD WON.
I WONDER HOW MANY MEN WE LOST IN THE BATTLE.
TWO MEN ARE MISSING, SIWARD. MACDUFF AND YOUR SON CANNOT BE FOUND.

I KNOW ABOUT ONE OF THEM. I AM SORRY TO SAY YOUNG SIWARD HAS BEEN KILLED.
AT LEAST HE DIED LIKE A SOLDIER!

JUST THEN, MACDUFF WALKED IN CARRYING THE HEAD OF MACBETH.
MACBETH IS DEAD. HAIL, MALCOLM, OUR RIGHTFUL KING!

AT THIS, THE THANES ALL HAILED MALCOLM AS THEIR NEW RULER.
THE BUTCHER, MACBETH, IS DEAD!
LET THERE BE PEACE IN THE LAND.
HAIL, MALCOLM!
HAIL! HAIL!
HAIL THE NEW KING OF SCOTLAND!
THE END